The
Snow
Queen

Hans Christian Andersen

Retold by Lesley Sims

Illustrated by
Alan Marks

Reading Consultant: Alison Kelly
University of Surrey Roehampton

Contents

Chapter 1

The magic mirror

There was once a wicked demon who made a magic mirror. This mirror made everything good look twisted and ugly. Anything bad looked even worse.

3

"It's a fine mirror," snarled the demon's students. "Let's show it off to the angels." Flapping their leathery wings, they flew up... and up... until...

s m a s h!

The mirror slipped from their hands, crashed to the ground and broke into a million tiny pieces.

Some pieces were no bigger than a grain of sand, but they were as powerful as the whole mirror. If a speck flew into someone's eye, everything looked horrible and wrong.

But if a splinter struck a person's heart, that heart began to freeze.

Chapter 2

Gerda and Kay

Not long after the mirror shattered, a girl named Gerda was living next door to a boy named Kay. In all the world, no two friends were as close.

One winter's day, as snow was falling, Gerda's grandmother told them the story of the Snow Queen.

"She lives in the icy north, but in winter she flies around, disguised as a snowflake."

"Beware of her!" the grandmother warned. "She's a wicked woman. But don't worry," she added. "If your heart is pure, you'll always see the queen for who she is."

7

Wandering home, Kay gazed
at the glittering snowflakes
drifting down. As he stared,
he noticed one flake
seemed larger than
the others.

Then he gasped. The snowflake
was definitely growing bigger...

...until it became a beautiful
woman. She was astonishing. Her
shimmering white clothes were
coated in snow and she herself
was made entirely of ice.

The Snow
Queen!

The woman turned her cold,
bright eyes on Kay. He shook his
head and she vanished. "I must
have imagined her," he thought.

Winter passed and Kay forgot all about the Snow Queen. Then one day, while he and Gerda watered the roses in her window box, Kay suddenly cried out.

He had felt a sharp jab in his eye and another, piercing his heart. But neither Kay nor Gerda could see what had happened.

The jabs came from splinters of the broken mirror. At once, Kay began to change and grow cruel.

Seeing Gerda's frightened face made him angry. He jumped up and left. Gerda listened sadly to his boots creaking down the stairs.

After that, Kay saw everything differently. He began to argue and make fun of people in the street. He even mocked Gerda and her roses, though she still loved him.

Next winter, Kay ignored Gerda altogether, and joined the boys on their sleds in the town square.

As they played, a dazzling white sleigh rode into the square. Its driver was dressed in white from her fur hat to her pointed boots.

Everyone but Kay ran away. He shouted, "This looks fun!" and tied his sled to the snow-white sleigh.

The two sharp splinters of mirror had blinded him to danger – for the driver was none other than the Snow Queen herself.

The sleigh picked up speed and Kay laughed with excitement. Hurtling around the square, they dashed out through the city gates.

On and on they flew, through
swirling snow. All too soon, the
sleigh stopped. As the driver stood
up, Kay realized who she was.

Quickly, the queen kissed Kay
and his icy heart grew colder. She
kissed him again and he forgot all
about home. He was trapped.

Chapter 3

Gerda's search

In town, no one knew where Kay
had gone. All through the cold,
dead winter, Gerda was too sad to
do anything. But when spring
came, with no sign of her best
friend, she decided to look for him.

"The river flows a long way," she thought. "Perhaps the river has passed him on its travels." Putting on her best, red shoes, she went down to the river.

If I give you my new red shoes, will you take me to Kay?

She threw her shoes into the river as a gift, but they floated back to her. So, she climbed into a boat to throw them further in... and the boat swept her away.

She floated for hours. Gerda was afraid but she couldn't turn back. She hoped the river would take her past someone who had seen Kay. But she saw no one.

As dusk fell, she spotted a rose-covered cottage. The boat began to drift to the bank and an old woman hobbled over.

You poor child! Are you lost?

The old woman helped Gerda onto the bank and Gerda told her all about Kay. She described their happy days playing until he suddenly changed.

First he grew mean. Then he disappeared altogether.

Now, the old woman wasn't wicked but she did know a little magic – and she lived a lonely life.

"I'll make sure the girl stays with me," she muttered and cast a spell.

To be extra sure, she made all her roses vanish. She didn't want to remind Gerda of the roses at home and her search for Kay.

Her magic worked. Gerda played happily in the woman's garden and her old life was soon no more real than a dream.

Even so, sometimes she had a feeling that something wasn't quite right...

Gerda might have stayed in the cottage forever but, one day, she spotted a painted flower on the woman's sunhat. It was a rose!

In that moment, Gerda remembered everything. "Kay!" she cried. "How could I forget you? Oh, I've wasted so much time!"

Without even saying goodbye to the old woman, she ran away.

Chapter 4

Kay in the castle

Meanwhile, the Snow Queen had taken Kay to her magnificent castle in the far north.

Kay was neither happy nor sad.
His feelings were frozen inside him.
He sat at the queen's feet, on a
vast icy lake, so cold he was
almost blue. But he didn't notice.

The queen sat sighing on her
throne, bored. Looking down on
Kay, she decided to play a game
with him. "Solve my puzzle and
I'll set you free," she declared.

Kay looked at her blankly.

The queen waved a pale hand at some blocks of ice. "If you put those in the right order, they will spell a word," she said, with a cruel smile.

Slowly, Kay's frozen brain realized she was telling him to spell something. He so wanted to please her but he just couldn't do it.

The Snow Queen laughed.
"You'll never do it, my icicle boy!"
she said. Her cold laugh bounced
off the walls of the castle. "But it's
amusing to watch you try..."

Chapter 5

A helpful princess

Gerda had run for hours to get away from the cottage, with no idea where she was going. At last, stumbling through a gloomy forest, she had to rest.

A curious crow hopped up to her, his head to one side. "Caw!" he croaked. "What are you doing, all alone in the world?"

I'm looking for my friend Kay. Have you seen him?

The crow listened to Gerda's story. "Caw, caw..." he said. "I think I might know where he is."

Gerda couldn't believe her luck. "Tell me!" she begged, excitedly.

"Well now," croaked the crow, "there's a princess in this kingdom and she was looking for a prince. In no time at all, men were lining up to meet her. But no one was good enough."

"Then a young boy appeared from nowhere. His clothes were torn and his boots creaked. But he went inside the palace and – would you believe it – the princess liked him so much, she married him!"

"That must be Kay!" Gerda cried. "He's handsome and clever... and his boots do squeak. Oh, please take me to him!"

"Caw. That's not so easily done," said the crow.

But Gerda pleaded and pleaded with him.

I'll speak to my wife. She works in the palace.

The crow flew off and Gerda waited nervously. Long after sunset, he returned – with good news. Trembling with hope, Gerda followed the crow to the palace. Inside, its grand rooms were draped in the purple night.

As they crept through the
ballroom, shadowy figures swept by.
"Who are they?" Gerda asked,
in a whisper.
"Dreams," replied the crow's wife.

They take the
royal thoughts for
midnight rides.

In the most splendid room of all, two giant flowers hung from a palm tree. The first flower had pure white petals and, curled up in the middle, lay the princess, fast asleep. The flower beside her was red.

Gerda stepped forward and looked in...

Kay? It's me, Gerda!

...and the prince woke up. "Who is it?" he mumbled.

Gerda stared at him and burst into tears. It wasn't Kay at all.

Gerda's noisy gulps and sobs woke the princess.

"Who are you?" she cried. Then, as Gerda didn't look dangerous, she gave her a hanky and let her sit down to explain.

That night, Gerda slept in the palace. In the morning, the princess gave Gerda her second-best dress and begged her to stay.

But all Gerda wanted was to search for Kay. "I'll walk around the world if I have to," she said.

The princess smiled and called for her carriage. Gerda gasped. It glistened with golden sugar and inside, the walls were lined with sticky buns and fat cream cakes.

For a second, she simply stared. "Is this really for me?" she asked, pointing to the golden carriage.

"Well, you can hardly walk around the whole world," said the princess, helping her climb in.

The carriage set off and Gerda waved through the window.

"Goodbye! Good luck!" cried the princess.

Chapter 6

The little robber girl

The carriage rolled on into a dark
forest. But it shone so brightly that
it dazzled a band of robbers, who
were hiding among the trees.

"Gold!" they shrieked and rushed
to attack.

"Mmm..." said an old robber woman, grabbing Gerda. "She looks tastier than the carriage. Let's eat her!" But, as she raised her knife, something sprang up and bit her ear.

It was the daughter of the chief robber – and she always got her own way.

"I want her for my friend," said the robber girl, pointing to Gerda, "and to play with her carriage."

"Hmph," said the old woman grumpily. The little robber girl pushed Gerda into the carriage and squashed in beside her.

Are you a princess?

No. I'm looking for my friend Kay.

As they rode deeper into the
forest, Gerda told her story yet
again. By nightfall, they arrived
at the robbers' grim,
lonely castle.

The little robber girl
yawned. "You can
sleep with me and
my pets," she
told Gerda.

Gerda frowned. The robber girl
had very strange pets. One hundred
pigeons roosted in the rafters and
two woodpigeons sat in a silver cage.
"They're all mine!" boasted
the little robber girl. "But
Ba is best of all." And she
pointed to a reindeer, who
was tied to the wall.

Say hello,
Ba!

"Bedtime!" she announced suddenly, flopping down. Gerda stayed awake, watching the robbers polish their knives around the fire. Things were worse than ever. She was stuck here, a prisoner again.

"I'll never find Kay," she sighed. Then the pigeons began talking.

Coo! Did you ever see such a frozen boy?

Coo! His face was like ice.

He'll never thaw now the Snow Queen has him.

"Could the Snow Queen have Kay?" wondered Gerda. "Please, where does the queen live?" she asked the pigeons politely.

"Somewhere north," they cooed. "Ask Ba if he knows."

The reindeer looked up. "Yes," he said, in a slow, deep voice. "I know her home. I'm from there too."

She lives in the far, far north, past Lapland.

The little robber girl, who was still awake, heard everything.

"You don't want to find that rotten old Snow Queen," she said. "You'd be safer here with us." But Gerda was desperate to find Kay.

"Then I shall let you go," said the robber girl, as proudly as a queen herself. "Ba shall take you."

"You'll need food," she went
on, finding Gerda bread and ham.
With a hard shove, she helped
Gerda on to the reindeer's silky-
smooth back.

Ba bounded off happily, racing
north to his home. The little robber
girl stood alone in the moonlight,
watching and waving until they
were out of sight.

Chapter 7

Journey north

It was a long way even to Lapland.
When they arrived, Ba and Gerda
were spotted by a Lapp woman.

"You're frozen!" she exclaimed to
Gerda, taking them into her hut.
"And you've a long way to go," she
added, when she heard their tale.

"You're in luck," she told them.
"The Snow Queen is away just now,
creating the Northern Lights. You
must go on to Finmark. I know a
Finn woman who can help."

Gerda watched in surprise as the
woman quickly scribbled a message
to her friend on a dried fish.

Ba galloped off once more across the snowy plains, until they reached the Finn woman's tiny hut.

First, the Finn woman read the fish. Then she listened as Gerda breathlessly told her tale. Nodding, she fetched a parchment from her shelves and studied it.

Finally, she took Ba to one side. "Kay *is* with the Snow Queen," she whispered. "He's under her spell, because of splinters of glass in his eye and his heart. To rescue him, Gerda must get the splinters out."

"But how?" growled Ba. "Can you give her some magic?"

"Gerda has come this far," said the Finn woman wisely. "She is good and sweet and innocent. That will be all the magic she needs."

"Take Gerda as far as the Snow Queen's garden," she went on. "But don't tell her what I've told you." She swept Gerda up and placed her on the reindeer's back.

Go quickly now!

I hope Ba knows where we're going.

Ba galloped until they reached a bush with glossy red berries. There, he stopped and let Gerda down.

Gerda was left all alone in the icy cold. Glittering snowflakes whirled around her, making it difficult for her to move. They were the guards of the Snow Queen's castle.

As she hesitated, the guards took on terrible shapes. Huge hedgehogs with vicious spikes, fang-toothed snakes and fierce bears sprang at her. Gerda cried out in fear, but she didn't run away.

Standing boldly before the guards,
she told them to leave her alone.
Her breath blew out in misty clouds
around her. To her astonishment,
these clouds became angels, who
began to attack the guards.

Seeing the angels gave Gerda strength. She punched the bear nearest to her and he melted at her touch. Then the angels warmed Gerda's icy feet and hands and she hurried into the castle.

Chapter 8

The snow castle

Inside a cold, empty hall, Kay
was puzzling over the Snow
Queen's challenge. He sat still,
thinking hard... so still that he
seemed frozen stiff.

And that was how Gerda found him, when she appeared moments later.

"Kay!" she called, running up to him. She wrapped her arms around him, but he didn't move.

Gerda didn't know what to do.
It was like hugging a block of ice.
He was frozen stiff and he didn't
even look at her.

Hot tears dripped from her nose
onto Kay's chest. They reached
right through to his heart, thawing
the ice and washing away the
splinter of glass.

Kay seemed to soften, so Gerda started to talk about the roses back home. Her words and his melting heart brought tears to Kay's eyes too... tears which washed away the splinter there.

He could see clearly again. "Gerda!" he shouted. "Is it really you?" The old Kay was back.

Gerda and Kay laughed and cried and jumped for joy. Even the blocks of ice around them got up and danced. When the blocks fell down again, they spelled the word "Eternity". Kay was free.

Gerda kissed his cheeks so that they glowed.

"Gerda! Yuck!" said Kay, but Gerda kept kissing him until he was completely thawed.

"Let's go!" begged Kay. "The Snow Queen could be back at any minute..."

"She's back now!" said an icy voice, behind them.

Kay and Gerda looked at each other in horror.

"You said if I spelled a word I was free," Kay shouted bravely, "and there it is! I'm going!"

The Snow Queen was furious but there was nothing she could do. She had given her word and she was bound by it.

Laughing with relief, Gerda and Kay tore outside the castle, to find Ba and a friend waiting for them. To Gerda's delight, the reindeer carried them all the way home.

At long last, they arrived at Gerda's house. Her grandmother had given up hope of ever seeing either of them again.

Is it really you? You defeated the Snow Queen?

Gerda and Kay hugged the grandmother over and over.

"This is truly a fairy-tale ending!" cried the grandmother and the roses in the window box nodded their heads, as if to agree.

Hans Christian Andersen was born in Denmark in 1805, the son of a poor shoemaker. He left home at fourteen to seek his fortune and became famous all over the world as a writer of fairy tales.

Designed by Russell Punter

First published in 2004 by Usborne Publishing Ltd., Usborne House, 83-85 Saffron Hill, London EC1N 8RT, England. www.usborne.com
Copyright © 2004 Usborne Publishing Ltd.